# THE STAR PEOPLE

## A Lakota Story

### S.D. NELSON

ABRAMS BOOKS FOR YOUNG READERS
NEW YORK

Young Wolf and I had wandered far across the prairie. Being his older sister, I wanted to show him the wonders of our world. "Look up, Brother. Do you see how Father Sun travels high in the sky during the day? And see beneath our feet? Mother Earth is alive with growing things." My little brother looked for a long moment, then said, "Sister Girl, I cannot see our village anymore."

"Let's stay for just a while longer, Young Wolf," I said. "Then we will go back."

We sat in the dry, sweet-smelling grass, watching the clouds drift overhead. Young Wolf pointed and said, "Sister Girl, that cloud looks like a buffalo's head!" We both laughed with amazement.

"There's an eagle!" I cried.

"And horses!" said Young Wolf.

"The cloud spirits are playing above us," I told my brother. "Sometimes they take the shapes of animals or people. The clouds are alive, and we call them the Cloud People."

As the Cloud People changed their shapes, the face of a woman emerged. "Look!" my brother gasped. "Grandmother!" Elk Tooth Woman had died that spring, and we missed her very much.

As I looked, I realized the clouds had turned dark in
the distance. Lightning struck the dry earth.

"The day is coming to an end," I told Young Wolf.
"Mother and Father will be expecting us."

Overhead, birds cried. Rabbits, deer, and other animals bounded past, their eyes wide with fear. Something was terribly wrong.

"I smell smoke!" said Young Wolf.

A prairie fire!

We joined the fleeing creatures and ran for our lives. "Mother! Father!" we cried. But our voices could not be heard above the roaring fire—and we had wandered so far from our village.

The flames were catching up to us. The smoke made it impossible to see. I stumbled down a hill, and Young Wolf fell behind me. Rolling down the hill, I despaired. We would never see our home again, or our mother and father . . . .

"Look, Brother," I said to Young Wolf who was softly
crying. "We are safe! Be glad. The fire did not catch us!"
    I coaxed him out of the water and up the bank. A strange
blackened land stretched before us. I knew that I had made
a mistake by wandering so far from home. Now I had no
idea how to find our village, and the dark of night was
near. I tried not to cry, but tears came to my eyes as I
comforted my brother.

"Sister Girl," Young Wolf said. "Sister Girl, the stars are dancing."

I looked up. High above us, the stars were becoming shapes, as the clouds had done that afternoon. First there was a coyote, then a bear, hawk, and many other creatures, both animal and human. Chanting, the Star People encircled us.

"They are the spirits of the Old Ones who once walked on this earth," I told my brother.

Young Wolf was first to see Elk Tooth Woman
dancing among them. "It's my Grandma!" he cried.

"You are safe now, my little Young Wolf," she
whispered, holding out her arms. "I am here, my
Sister Girl."

I was delighted to see our grandmother. Young
Wolf was happy, but confused.  He said,
"Grandma, I thought I would never see you again."

Smiling, she drew us close to her, tenderly
rocking back and forth.  Beneath a heaven full of
stars we fell into a deep sleep.

In our dream, raindrops pattered upon the burned
ground. Wildflowers grew, and crickets chirped.
Moths fluttered about in the cool moonlight. Creatures
crawled from the safety of their burrows—badger,
lizard, turtle, rabbit.

The wild ones gathered in a circle. Dancing, they
chanted a joyous song.

*Thank you, raindrops, the fire is gone.*
*Thank you, Sister Moon, the fire is gone.*
*Hey yah hey!*
*Star People above, we are alive.*
*Hey yah hey!*

In our dream, Grandmother and Young Wolf lifted
their feet to the beat of the drum. I joined in their dance.
Together, we all gave thanks.

In the morning, when we awoke, I felt an emptiness in my heart.
I missed our parents.

Young Wolf felt the emptiness of his stomach. "I'm hungry!"
he said.

Elk Tooth Woman laughed. She took us to a place where berry
bushes had escaped the fire. We ate our fill. Then Grandmother
said she would take us home.

We traveled a long time across the barren land. In places there
were flowers and green grass, untouched by the fire. That was a
sign of hope.

Finally we came to a hilltop. Looking down, Young Wolf howled, "There's our village!"

I turned to Grandmother. "Our mother and father will be so happy to see you again."

She shook her head. "I can go no farther. I must return to my home in the sky."

Young Wolf clutched Elk Tooth Woman and would not let her go. Tears streamed down his round cheeks. I pleaded with her to stay. Drawing away from us, Grandmother smiled and said, "Don't worry, my Sister Girl, my Young Wolf. I will always be with you. The Star People are always with you. Look up, and you will see me among the stars."

So Young Wolf and I returned home
safely. Our parents wept with joy to
see their children—and then they were
very angry with us for wandering so far
from home.

But ever after, when my little brother
and I walked beneath the star-filled
heavens, we felt comfort. For we knew
our grandmother and all of the Star
People were watching over us.

Growing up in the 1950s, I was told magical stories about the Star People. I also heard true-life stories about my great-great-grandfather, whose name was Flying Cloud. My mother, whose Indian name was Elk Tooth Woman, was born and raised on the Dakota prairies. She was bilingual, speaking both English and Sioux. She taught me how to look at the moon and stars above and how to "see" Mother Earth and Father Sky as being *Wakan*, or sacred. I learned that there is a spirit within all things known as *Wakan Tanka*, the Great Mystery. My father, a career army officer of Norwegian descent, embraced the Indian ways and, in the turn of the circle, was fully accepted by my mother's family.

In the late 1800s the U.S. Government demanded that the Plains Indian tribes move onto tracts of land called reservations. Many of the warriors resisted. Individuals believed to be the leaders of any such resistance were imprisoned. Eventually, overwhelmed and literally starving, for the great buffalo herds were completely gone, all of the Native Americans yielded. Following that, their children were forced to attend government boarding schools. During their incarceration, these people developed a unique art style known as ledger book art. Using pens, colored pencils, and crayons, they made drawings on the lined paper of discarded accounting books called ledger books. With simple bold shapes and vivid colors they depicted village scenes, battles, ceremonials, and even their imprisonment. The figures of people and horses are mostly drawn in profile. Their images are laid down directly upon lined pages previovsly covered with bookkeeping records. Visually, the Indian images float above the lined paper of the "white man" with its written words. Sadly, and in the most compelling manner, the intentions of the bookkeeper and the Indian artist oppose one another; the two cultures never seem to connect. *The Star People* is set on the Great Plains during this period. The pictures were done with acrylic paint on heavy watercolor paper, in a style that is a contemporary interpretation of this traditional Lakota art.

Color has great symbolism for Native Americans. They decorated their tipis, their horses, and even themselves to "capture" the spirit-power possessed by certain colors. Red, for example, represents the first of the four sacred directions—East, the dawn, and the power of a warrior. Likewise, to obtain power from the elements, they tied hawk and eagle feathers in their hair. It was believed this would give a person the spirit-power of the great flying birds.

Cloud People and Star People are, in fact, the traditional Lakota way of referring to clouds and stars. They have a living energy, just like

A traditional Lakota drawing from the Red Hawk ledger book (circa 1880s). *Steals Goverment* [sic] *Horse and Saddle*, pencil, ink, and crayon on paper, 7 1/2 x 12 1/4 inches, courtesy of the Milwaukee Public Museum.

people. Likewise, four-legged creatures and winged beings are considered equals and are often personified as people.

The character of Sister Girl is based on a real person. "Sister Girl" was the childhood nickname of my favorite cousin; being older, she was more like an aunt to me. She was born and raised on the Standing Rock Reservation in the Dakotas. Her name was given to her by my mother and grandmother.

The name Elk Tooth Woman is an honorable one. It refers to the ivory teeth of the majestic elk, which were considered rare and very beautiful. They were used to decorate women's dresses just like the one worn by the grandmother in this story. In time, glass trade beads replaced them as adornments for clothing.

Today, as an adult and a member of the Standing Rock Sioux Tribe, it is my pleasure to pass on traditional Lakota teachings to young readers. It is my hope that their lives might be enriched by this different world view.

---

*For my parents, Elk Tooth Woman and The Grizz, whose spirits*
*dance together with the Star People above the Dakota prairies.*
—S.D.

ACKNOWLEDGMENTS

I am indebted to the many scholars and artists who, through their personal dedication, have recorded the history of the Lakota/Sioux. Among them are Colin F. Taylor, Amos Bad Heart Buffalo, George Catlin, Howling Wolf, Janet Catherine Berlo, John Neihardt (for preserving the teachings of Black Elk, the Oglala Sioux medicine man), Mari Sandoz, and Benjamin Capps. And I am especially grateful to my wife, Karen, who assured me that *The Star People* was a story worth telling.

Designer: Becky Terhune

Library of Congress Cataloging-in-Publication Data
Nelson, S. D.
The Star People / by S. D. Nelson.
p. cm.
Summary: When Young Wolf and his older sister wander from their village and face the danger of a prairie fire, their deceased grandmother, now one of the Star People, appears to guide them.
ISBN 978-0-8109-4584-5
[1. Brothers and sisters—Fiction. 2. Grandmothers—Fiction. 3. Grassland fires—Fiction. 4. Stars—Fiction. 5. Indians of North America—Great Plains—Fiction.] I. Title.

PZ7.N4367St 2003
[E]—dc21
2002156367

Printed in China
15 14 13

Abrams Books for Young Readers are available at special discounts when purchased in quantity for premiums and promotions as well as fundraising or educational use. Special editions can also be created to specification. For details, contact specialsales@abramsbooks.com or the address below.

ABRAMS The Art of Books
195 Broadway, New York, NY 10007
abramsbooks.com

This edition published by Parragon Books Ltd in 2015

Parragon Books Ltd
Chartist House
15–17 Trim Street
Bath BA1 1HA, UK
www.parragon.com

*Olaf's Perfect Summer Day* and *Olaf's New Reindeer Friend* written by Jessica Julius
*Olaf and the Troll Tots* written by Brittany Candau
All stories illustrated by the Disney Storybook Art Team

ISBN 978-1-4748-1239-9

Printed in China

From the movie

Disney

# FROZEN

# OLAF's AMAZING ADVENTURES

Three tales to enjoy...

*Olaf's Perfect Summer Day*
*Olaf's New Reindeer Friend*
*Olaf and the Troll Tots*

PaRragon

Bath · New York · Cologne · Melbourne · Delhi
Hong Kong · Shenzhen · Singapore · Amsterdam

# OLAF's
## Perfect
## Summer Day

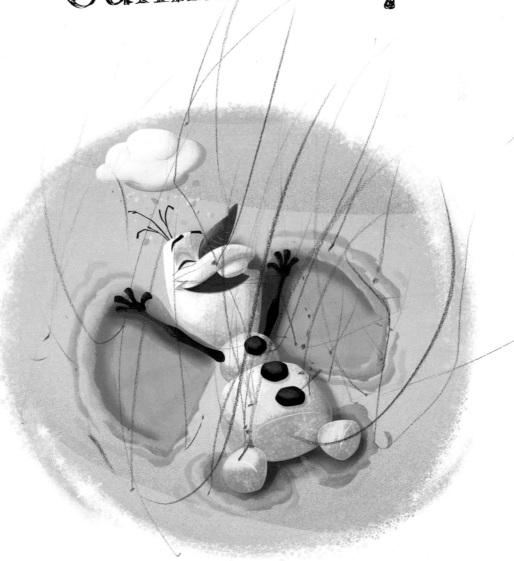

Summer had finally arrived in Arendelle. Everyone in the kingdom was enjoying the long, sunny days after a very cold winter season.

But today was going to be the hottest day of the year so far! Most of the villagers wanted to stay inside where it was cool.

But Olaf could hardly wait to get outside!
This was the kind of day he had always
dreamed about!

Olaf ran into Princess Anna's room, calling out happily.
"Anna, Anna! Guess what today is! It's the perfect
summery day! Let's go outside and play!"
Anna groaned as she sat up in bed. "It's too hot, Olaf!"
But she had to smile when she saw Olaf's hopeful face.

Together, Olaf and Anna went to look for Queen Elsa.
They found her in the Great Hall.

"There you are, Elsa!" Olaf cried out joyfully.

Olaf looked up shyly at the important-looking
visitor who was standing with Elsa.

"Hi, my name is Olaf and I like warm hugs."

"H-h-hello," the visitor stammered in surprise.
He had never seen a talking snowman before!

Olaf turned back to Elsa. "And today is the best day for warm hugs because it's sunny and hot. Please, can we go and play in the sunshine?"

Elsa laughed. "That sounds like fun, Olaf. What did you have in mind?"

"It's so hot, though," Anna interrupted. "Couldn't you cool things down just a bit, Elsa?" She looked hopefully at her sister.

"Olaf's always wanted to experience heat," said Elsa.
"Shouldn't we give him his special day? We'll do everything
he's always wanted to do in summer!"

"You're right, Elsa," agreed Anna. "How about a picnic
on the shores of the fjord?"

Olaf clasped his hands with glee. "Oooh, I love picnics!"

Anna, Elsa and Olaf headed to the royal kitchen to collect some picnic supplies. They found the cook with her head in the icebox!

"Olina, what on earth are you doing?" asked Elsa.

The cook popped her head up. "Trying to keep cool. It's so terribly hot!"

Olaf chuckled. "Did you bake cookies today?"

The cook shook her head. "Oh, it's too hot for baking."

Elsa glanced at Olaf. She didn't want him to miss out. "How about an ice-cold lemonade instead?" she suggested.

Olaf was thrilled. "Oooh, I love lemonade!"

Olaf, Anna and Elsa set off for their picnic.

In the royal gardens, a few children were lying on the grass. Olaf didn't realize they were too hot to play games. He ran over to them, giggling happily.

"Hi, my name is Olaf. Don't you just love summer?" The children liked Olaf, so they joined him in chasing butterflies and blowing fuzz off dandelions.

Even Elsa and Anna couldn't resist joining in!

After a while, Anna plopped herself down on the grass.
"Whew! I'm ready for our picnic!" she said.

Elsa agreed. "Yes, let's head to the docks. We can sail
to the fjord."

Olaf, who had been chasing a bumblebee, stopped in
his tracks. "We're going sailing? I've always
wanted to try sailing!"

At the docks, Anna and Elsa chose a beautiful sailing boat. As they set sail, Olaf hummed a happy tune. He even got to steer the boat for a while!

When they reached the shore, Olaf couldn't sit still!
"Don't you just love the feeling of sand on
your snow?" he squealed. "Let's make sand angels!"
Anna gingerly stuck a toe in the hot sand.
"Oh, goodness, that is ... warm!" she cried.

Anna danced on tiptoe over the hot sand to the
fjord's edge. "Ah, this is better," she said, as the cool
water washed over her feet.

The three friends spent the whole afternoon
playing in the summer sun.

They built sandcastles and sand people.

They chased waves on the shore
and even danced with seagulls!

And finally, when they'd tired themselves out, they sat down and had a wonderful picnic on the shores of the fjord.

"Hands down, this is the best day of my life," said Olaf.

As they sailed back to Arendelle, the setting sun made beautiful colours in the sky. Olaf was amazed. "I wish I could hug the summer sun. I bet it would feel wonderful!"

Anna smiled as she swept her sweaty hair off her face. "You might need a bigger snow flurry for that, Olaf!"

The trio soon reached the dock, where Kristoff and Sven were waiting to greet them. Everyone was tired after the hot day – apart from Olaf, who couldn't stop talking about the picnic!

"Summer is wonderful," Elsa said with a wink. "But tomorrow, I predict a chance of snow."

## THE END

# OLAF'S
## New Reindeer Friend

Princess Anna and Queen Elsa were working hard to prepare for the kingdom's first ball since Elsa's magical powers had been revealed. The people of Arendelle had accepted Elsa and her magic, and the sisters wanted to thank them with a special celebration.

"I want the people to know we care," Elsa said. "I want this ball to be different from anything they've ever seen!"

"Oh, Elsa," said Anna. "Just having a ball is special enough!"

"I agree, Your Majesty," said a servant, entering the room.

The kindly servant looked around.
"Hmm ... crocus flowers would be nice for
the centrepieces."

"That's true, but everything already looks beautiful,"
Anna said. "The party is tonight, Elsa, and you need
a break. Besides, I want to spend some time with you!"

"I'd love to," replied Elsa. "But what about the crocuses?"

"Well," said Anna, thinking quickly, "let's gather them ourselves! We'll be doing something useful *and* spending time together."

"What a good idea!" said Elsa. "And Olaf can help, too."

Anna and Elsa found Olaf
just outside the castle.

"Hello, Olaf!" said Anna.
"We're going to look for crocuses.
Will you help us?"

Olaf clapped his hands.
"Ooooh! I love crocuses!"

Anna, Elsa and Olaf walked into the mountains and played all day long.

They enjoyed having fun outside of the castle walls!

"Maybe our party should be fancy dress!" Anna suggested, giggling.

"That's right, the ball!" said Elsa. She had almost forgotten about it. "Don't forget, we still need a lot more crocuses!"

As they walked further along the path, Anna spotted
Wandering Oaken's Trading Post and Sauna.

"Look! I remember this place," cried Anna. "I bet
Oaken will have something for our ball."

Olaf couldn't wait to see inside!

"Hoo-hoo!" called Oaken as they entered the shop.

"Hello! Do you have anything special for a ball?" asked Anna.

"My big winter blowout is special. Half price shoes for walking on snow! Or karts for sliding down mountains!" Oaken exclaimed.

Outside, Elsa looked at Anna's sledge full of shopping. "Those things aren't very useful for the ball," she said.

"I know," Anna grinned. "But he was so nice, how could I say no?"

Elsa laughed. As they set out again, Olaf ran ahead, shouting, "This is the best day of my life!"

Soon the group found lots more crocuses.
Elsa gasped. "They're beautiful!"
While the girls collected flowers, Olaf chased a bee.
All was well until ...

... Olaf nearly ran off the edge of a cliff!

"Hang on there, Olaf!" exclaimed Elsa,
using her magic to stop him falling over the edge.

But Olaf didn't even notice. "Look at that!"
he said, staring at something below. It was a young
reindeer trapped on a ledge.

"How did you get down there?" Anna asked.
"And how will we get you back up?"

Elsa thought for a moment.
Then she waved her hands.
Suddenly, a ramp of ice sprang
magically into the air and
stretched down onto the ledge.

"Whoa," said Olaf.
"Now the little reindeer
can climb out!"

Carefully, the reindeer stepped on to the ice ramp ... but it was too slippery!

"Now what?" asked Elsa.

"I know!" said Anna. She grabbed the shopping she had bought at Oaken's Trading Post, jumped onto the ramp and slid down to join the little reindeer on the ledge.

First, Anna pulled out the snowshoes.
"I knew these would be useful," she said,
fitting them on the reindeer.

Then she tied a rope round the reindeer
and threw it to Elsa. "Pull!" Anna shouted.

Elsa and Olaf pulled on the rope together.

At last, everyone was safely at the top!

"Can we invite the reindeer to the ball?" asked Olaf.

"The ball!" Anna and Elsa shouted together. They needed to get back to the castle!

Elsa grabbed Anna's and Olaf's hands and led them to the kart. "Hold on!" she said. Using her magic, Elsa created snow slide after snow slide, and they slid all the way down the mountain.

When they arrived at the palace, Elsa, Anna, Olaf and the little reindeer landed right in the middle of the ballroom! Crocus flowers rained down on the guests, who were delighted by the grand entrance.

"See?" said Anna. "Nobody has ever seen a ball like this before!"
Elsa laughed. "And best of all, we're all enjoying it together!"

# THE END

# OLAF
## and the
## Troll Tots

Anna, Kristoff and Sven were heading towards the setting sun. They were off to Troll Valley to babysit the toddler trolls while the adults went to their annual magic convention.

"I wonder if I should have brought games," Anna said. "Do trolls like games?"

"Oh, don't worry," Kristoff replied. "They'll probably be sleeping the whole time. I bet we'll just be relaxing by the fire and maybe eating some snacks."

He explained that Bulda, his adoptive troll mother, had a very strict bedtime for all the young trolls. Sven grunted in agreement.

They reached Troll Valley and were greeted warmly by the trolls.

"It seems like just yesterday you were young enough to have a babysitter yourself, Kristoff," said Bulda. "All you wanted to do was run naked through the valley!"

"Oh, really?" Anna asked, stifling a giggle.

"Okay, that's enough stories for now," Kristoff said.

Bulda took Anna and Kristoff to the troll tots.

"If they get hungry, you can feed them smashed berries.
And they may need a leaf change. But it's just about their
bedtime, so they should be sleeping soon."

As the adult trolls headed off, Anna waved goodbye.
"Have a great time! Everything is going to be fine...."

But everything wasn't fine!

As soon as the adult trolls left, the toddlers escaped from their pen. They were running, climbing and swinging all over the place!

"Oh no, no," Anna said, rushing to help a few tots who were climbing the boulders. "That's dangerous."

Kristoff ran to a leaning tower of troll tots that
had just sprouted.

"All right, guys," Kristoff said, gently pulling the
trolls off one another. "Let's settle down now."

But the more that Kristoff and Anna tried to calm
the little trolls, the wilder they became!

"Maybe they're hungry!" Anna said, heading for the basket of smashed berries.

"Yummy!" she cooed. But the trolls clearly felt they had better things to do.

"Maybe they need changing?" Kristoff said, bravely peering into one of the trolls' nappy leaves. "Nope!"

"Let's put them to bed," Anna suggested. "They must be tired by now."

But the young trolls were wide awake.

Suddenly, a cheery voice interrupted them.
"Hello, troll babies!"
It was Olaf!

"Elsa sent me in case you needed some help,"
Olaf explained as the tots clambered all over him.
"Why, hi there. Ha ha! That tickles!" Olaf was a
real hit with the little trolls!

"Boy, are we glad to see you," Kristoff said.

Anna ran to greet the snowman. But in her hurry, she tripped, falling face-first into the basket of berries!

"Whoaaa!" she yelled.

Kristoff rushed to her side. "Anna! Are you okay?"

Anna lifted her head, her face covered in dripping purple goop. The little trolls burst into loud giggles. They leaped up and started lapping up the berry juice from her cheeks!

Anna laughed. "Well, I guess that's one way to feed them."

After the trolls had finished all the berry juice, they sat in a row, happy and full. But suddenly, a strange smell floated into the air. The trolls looked down at their leaves.

"Uh-oh," Kristoff said, realizing what had happened. "Olaf, you distract them."

Olaf happily told the little trolls stories about his favourite thing in the world – summer. Anna and Sven collected new leaves while Kristoff changed the nappies. Soon everyone was clean and sweet-smelling once more!

"And now for my show-stopping song about summer!" Olaf announced.

Anna noticed that some of the tots were having trouble keeping their eyes open.

"Actually," she said, "maybe Kristoff would like to sing a lullaby instead."

So Kristoff played while Anna and Olaf put the trolls to bed. By the time the adult trolls returned, the little ones were sound asleep.

"Wow, great job," Bulda whispered.

"It was easy," Anna replied, winking at Kristoff. "But we couldn't have done it without Olaf."

**THE END**